HALLOWEENSCAPES

JESSICA MAZURKIEWICZ

DOVER PUBLICATIONS, INC.
GARDEN CITY, NEW YORK

NOTE

Add some tricks and treats to the Halloween season with this coloring book featuring full-page patterns created from traditional imagery. Highlights include witches on broomsticks, haunted houses, vampires, Halloween candy, black cats, goblins, ghouls, and more! Each pattern is enclosed inside a detailed border for a finished look. The 30 black-and-white images created by artist Jessica Mazurkiewicz will make a distinctive holiday project for colorists of all ages. Just add color with crayons, markers, or colored pencils and add your own unique touch to these festive holiday designs.

Copyright

Copyright © 2011 by Dover Publications, Inc.
All rights reserved.

Bibliographical Note

HalloweenScapes is a new work, first published by Dover Publications, Inc., in 2011.

International Standard Book Number

ISBN-13: 978-0-486-48179-1
ISBN-10: 0-486-48179-4

Manufactured in the United States by LSC Communications
48179408   2020
www.doverpublications.com

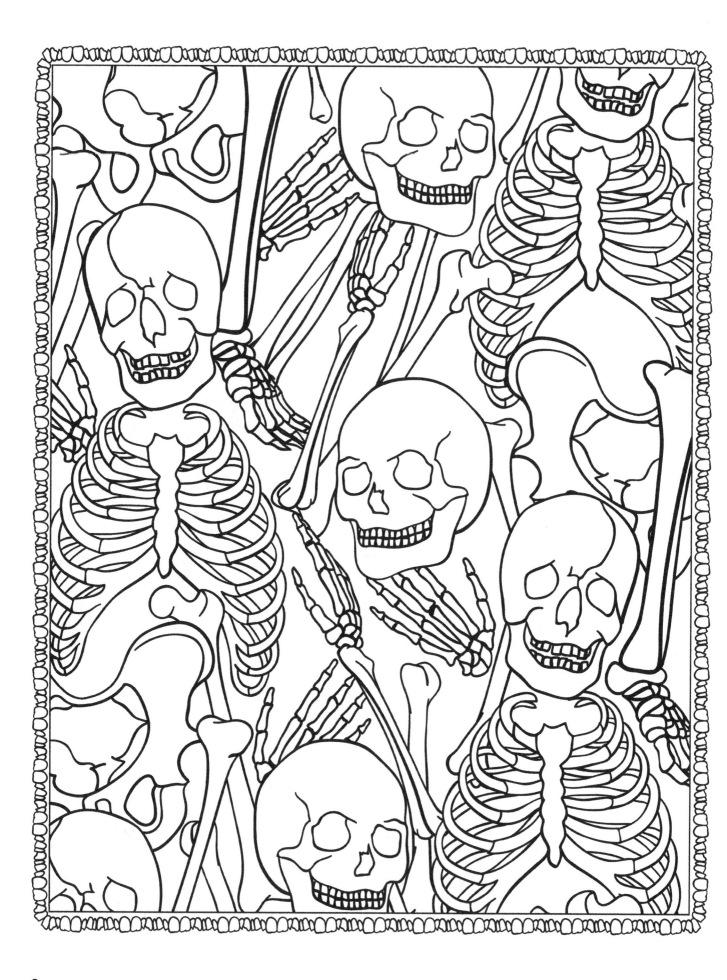

5

6

9

10

13

15

16

17

28